DATE DUE

1993	

PRINTED IN U.S.A.

The
Wilsons

by
Cass R. Sandak

CRESTWOOD HOUSE
New York

Maxwell Macmillan Canada
Toronto

Maxwell Macmillan International
New York   Oxford   Singapore   Sydney

Library of Congress Cataloging-in-Publication Data
Sandak, Cass R.
   The Wilsons / by Cass R. Sandak. — 1st ed.
      p.   cm. — (First families)
   Includes bibliographical references and index.
   Summary: A biography of Woodrow Wilson, with emphasis on his years as president. The book tells the story of the only president who had two first ladies: Ellen Axson Wilson and Edith Bolling Wilson.
   ISBN 0-89686-651-3
   1. Wilson, Woodrow, 1856–1924—Juvenile literature. 2. Wilson, Ellen Axson, 1860–1914—Juvenile literature. 3. Wilson, Edith Bolling Galt, 1872–1961—Juvenile literature. 4. Presidents—United States—Biography—Juvenile literature. 5. Presidents—United States—Wives—Biography—Juvenile literature.
   I. Title. II. Series: Sandak, Cass R.   First families.
E767.S23   1993
973.91'3'092—dc20
[B]   93-3503

Photo Credits
All photos courtesy of The Bettmann Archive.

CRESTWOOD HOUSE

Macmillan Publishing Company
866 Third Avenue
New York, NY 10022

Maxwell Macmillan Canada, Inc.
1200 Eglinton Avenue East
Suite 200
Don Mills, Ontario M3C 3N1

Macmillan Publishing Company is part of the Maxwell Communication Group of Companies.

Produced by Flying Fish Studio

Printed in the United States of America

First edition

10 9 8 7 6 5 4 3 2 1

Contents

In 1917 the United States entered World War I. Many American soldiers gave their lives fighting for peace.

A World at War

World War I had begun in Europe in 1914. German soldiers had marched into Belgium. No part of Europe seemed safe from the enemy.

From the beginning, President Woodrow Wilson had been strongly against U.S. involvement in the war. And the country had managed to stay out of the fighting until 1917. But then, however, German ships began harassing American vessels on the high seas. Earlier, the great British liner *Lusitania* had been sunk without warning in May of 1915. Of the 1,198 lives lost, 128 were Americans.

It was becoming more and more clear that America would have to enter the fighting. On April 2, 1917, President Wilson asked Congress to declare war. Four days later Wilson signed a declaration of war that finally brought the United States into combat. Within months five million Americans were bearing arms—most of them soldiers dispatched to the battlefields of Europe. Americans fought in the war for only one year, but the effect was still devastating.

Wilson's rallying cry for entrance into World War I was "to make the world safe for democracy." It was a lofty ideal. The conflict was also to be "the war to end all wars." Sadly, it wasn't. Moreover, it initiated the condition of the modern world, in which nations appear always to be on the brink of war. Since 1914 there has been almost continual conflict in some location or other, sometimes flaring into outright war.

World War I is one of the great watersheds of history. Many historians have said that the 19th century did not end until 1914. Others call the war the end of the old world. For some writers World War I marks the dividing line between "history" and modern times.

The war was significant for many reasons. It was the time when the world lost its innocence. It marked the end of an era. When the war started, soldiers clamored to sign up for what seemed like a noble and exciting adventure. By the war's end, millions of people—soldiers and civilians—were dead or maimed. More lives were lost than in any previous war, as a result of newer, more dangerous weapons and the widespread nature of the conflict. No one would ever again think that war was glamorous.

No one thought that the Civil War was glamorous either. It had taken place within one country, although one divided. One of Woodrow Wilson's earliest memories dated from around 1860, when he was about four years old. He was playing in the front garden of the family home in Augusta, Georgia, when a man passed by. The man told young Wilson two things. He said that Abraham Lincoln had been elected president. He also told the young boy that there would be a war. The man's prophecy came true and was to prove one of the great formative experiences of young Wilson's life.

Young Wilson

Wilson was born in Staunton, Virginia, on December 28, 1856. In fact, Wilson was born shortly after midnight, which would make December 29 his birthdate. But his family always celebrated his birthday on December 28.

The youngster was named Thomas Woodrow Wilson, and for about the first 20 years of his life Wilson was known as Tommy. His father, Joseph Ruggles Wilson, was minister of the First Presbyterian Church in Staunton.

Woodrow Wilson's birthplace in Staunton, Virginia

Wilson's mother was named Janet Woodrow, although she was called Jessie most of her life. Wilson had two older sisters, Marion and Annie.

Young Wilson was born in the spacious and attractive minister's home of the Presbyterian church in Staunton. He spent only a year of his young life in the Old Dominion State, but it was enough time for him always to consider himself a Virginian.

In 1858 the Wilsons moved to Augusta, Georgia, where Joseph Wilson became minister of the First Presbyterian Church. Most of Wilson's youth was spent in Georgia and South Carolina.

Wilson's ancestors were Scottish and Scots-Irish. His grandparents had all been born abroad, and so had his mother. The Woodrows, his mother's family, had emigrated from England when Jessie was nine. The winter crossing was a particularly rough one during which Jessie was nearly swept overboard.

Both sides of the family were staunchly Presbyterian. One grandfather and Wilson's own father were members of the clergy. His other grandfather was in newspaper publishing and politics. For a time it seemed that Woodrow himself was destined for the church. Both his parents hoped that the young boy would make religion his life's work, but he surprised—and disappointed—them. Throughout his life Wilson remained a committed Christian, but he found his calling in spheres outside the church—scholarship, teaching, and politics.

Born shortly before the Civil War began, Wilson was old enough to witness its events as a wide-eyed, impressionable child. Wilson was four when the Civil War began and eight when it ended. He remembered few incidents of the war but received many impressions of the struggle: the anxiety, the fear, the frantic activity, the futility, the grief.

The war that divided the nation also divided the Wilson family. Some close relatives were officers or soldiers in the Union army, while others were in the Confederate army. Young Wilson himself sympathized with the Southern cause but believed that the war was necessary to preserve the unity of the nation.

Most of Augusta had been reduced to rubble in the wake of the retreating Union army. Wilson had early memories of prisoners being brought into the family church in Augusta. It was a common sight for the wounded to be treated in churches because there were not enough hospitals.

Tommy Goes to School

Young Tommy Wilson was taught at home until he was nine years old. Only then did he receive formal schooling. He was a reluctant learner, possibly because of dyslexia (a reading disorder). Or he may also have been a silent rebel against subtle family pressures. He did not master the alphabet until he was nine, and it was several more years until he could read with ease and interest. It should be noted that Wilson was not alone among great men in being "slow" as a child. Both Albert Einstein and the Irish poet William Butler Yeats, for example, shared this "defect."

The Wilsons had their last child in 1866. He was named Joseph Ruggles Wilson, Jr., after his father. And in 1870 the family made another move. This time they went to Columbia, South Carolina, where Rev. Wilson was assigned to the First Presbyterian Church. In addition, he was to spend part of his time teaching at the seminary in Columbia. Largely destroyed by the Civil War, Columbia was not a pleasant place in which to live.

In Columbia, Wilson went to a private school. Although a bright youngster, Tommy was not a particularly distinguished scholar. He had a pleasing tenor voice and was a member of the chorus or glee club. He also developed a stirring speaking voice, which would serve him well in his later life. About this time he began to use both his brain and his speaking skills to become a noted debater.

Wilson at College

At 16, Wilson enrolled at Davidson College, a religious school. Wilson decided that he would follow his father and go into the ministry. But he lasted only a year at Davidson. Frail health forced him to leave the school and return home. By this time the family had moved to Wilmington, North Carolina.

After a period of recovery, Wilson transferred to Princeton University. (The school was known as the College of New Jersey until it was renamed Princeton in 1896.)

The university was an old and famous one. It was the elder Wilson's alma mater, and Wilson's father had graduated at the top of his class.

During his years at Princeton, Wilson continued to pursue his interests at his own pace. He was recognized by his classmates as a brilliant student, but his grades were undistinguished. His father was particularly disappointed in Wilson's academic performance. On graduation day in 1879, Wilson felt the sting of not fulfilling all his father's expectations. He took no part in the orations and other ceremonies of the day but simply received his degree.

Woodrow Wilson at the time he graduated from Princeton

By now Wilson knew that a life in the church was not for him. Through debating, he had become aware of politics and decided that government service would be a good place for him to cast his lot. As a result, law school seemed to be the next logical step. Accordingly, in the fall of 1879 Wilson enrolled at the University of Virginia Law School. There he excelled at speechmaking and polished his talent as an orator.

About this time, at his mother's urging, Wilson dropped the "Tommy" in his name. Wilson was already in his early 20s. Woodrow had been his middle name and his mother's family name. And Woodrow Wilson would be the name by which the man became a world figure.

While he was in law school, Wilson fell in love for the first time with his cousin, Hattie Woodrow, who was attending school nearby. Wilson's parents were not overjoyed at such a close relationship, but they supported the couple. In the end, Hattie rejected Woodrow, and nothing ever came of the match.

Wilson never graduated from law school. He left the University of Virginia due to poor health. He continued to study on his own and in October 1882 he passed the bar exam. Then Wilson and a friend set up a law office in Atlanta, Georgia. Although promising at first, the practice was never very successful. Wilson wasn't particularly bothered, since he saw law merely as a stepping stone to politics.

A photo of the young Ellen Axson

Ellen Axson

In April of 1883 Wilson went to visit some cousins in Rome, Georgia. While attending a church service there, he met an astonishing young woman. Her name was Ellen Louise Axson. Born in Savannah, Georgia, in 1860, she too was a child of a minister.

Dissatisfied with law, Wilson felt he needed further schooling. He enrolled at the newly established Johns Hopkins University in Baltimore, Maryland. While Wilson was in Baltimore, Ellen Axson was in New York City. There she followed her natural talent as an artist and studied painting. Wilson studied government and history and found time to sing in the glee club and form debate societies. He also made frequent trips to New York to visit Ellen.

The two were unofficially engaged in 1883, and although they were separated by distance, the couple wrote intimate letters to each other almost daily. Nearly all the correspondence between the couple survives. The letters reveal an incredibly passionate and romantic man who seems somehow at odds with the image of the stern leader.

A New Life

While still at Johns Hopkins, Wilson began to write a book. He wanted to make use of his intellectual skills. When he was 28, the book was published. Called *Congressional Government: A Study in American Politics*, it was very successful. Unlike many academic books, this one reached a wider public and for a while helped increase Wilson's income. Wilson received his graduate degree—a doctor of philosophy, or Ph.D. Wilson submitted *Congressional Government* as his dissertation.

On June 24, 1885, Woodrow Wilson and Ellen Axson were married at Ellen's grandfather's home in Savannah, Georgia. Woodrow was 28, Ellen was 25. Ellen's grandfather and Woodrow's father jointly performed the ceremony.

That fall the newlyweds moved to Pennsylvania, where Wilson had accepted a teaching post at Bryn Mawr College. The brand-new school had been founded by Quakers and was designed to give a first-class education to women only. It was Wilson's first teaching job.

The Wilsons had very small quarters in one of the college's small buildings. Because of the lack of space, they were unable to entertain a great deal. Although Ellen Wilson was a poised and delightful hostess, the couple generally kept to themselves. Necessity formed a pattern that they would keep as long as they were married. Because Wilson was making some extra money from the sales of his book, the Wilsons were soon able to move to slightly larger quarters. But they still led a quiet life.

Thoughtful, reserved, well-read and brilliant, Ellen Wilson resented the demands of public life because they made inroads on her time for family and intellectual pursuits. She later said that the happiest years of her marriage were those spent when Wilson was teaching in the history department at Bryn Mawr College.

A short, round-faced woman, Ellen Wilson cared little for external things. She herself admitted that she was not ambitious. She was loved by her family and staff and indeed by all with whom she came into contact.

In April of 1886 their first daughter, Margaret, was born. She was followed in August of 1887 by a sister, Jessie Woodrow.

Ellen Wilson was the perfect match for her husband. Like most women of the time, she kept the house and took care of the children. But Mrs. Wilson was smart, and she also helped her husband in his endeavors. She proofread all his writing and edited many of his speeches.

Although teaching at Bryn Mawr was a successful experiment, news of Wilson's talents traveled. As a result, he received an offer from Wesleyan University, in Middletown, Connecticut. The Wilsons moved there in 1888. Their third and last daughter, Eleanor Randolph, was born in Middletown in October 1889.

Even Wesleyan could not satisfy Wilson's desire to sharpen his abilities. When Wilson was asked to return to Princeton to teach law and political economy in 1890, he could not resist the offer.

In 1902 Wilson was named president of Princeton University. He was just 46 years old. Before Wilson, every president of the distinguished school had been a Presbyterian minister. Wilson was the first Princeton president who had not been professionally involved with the church.

Wilson worked hard to make Princeton one of the best colleges in the country. Before his time, the school had the reputation of being just for rich students. From Wilson's time on, the university became a truly distinguished home of fine scholarship, and it has remained so to the present day.

Into Politics

Wilson had always felt that he belonged in politics, but so far his accomplishments identified him mainly as a distinguished scholar and speaker. But powerful leaders had watched Wilson's rise and saw his ability to take on larger roles.

In 1910 Wilson's name was put on the ballot as the Democratic candidate for governor of New Jersey. Running for governor was a major risk. Although Wilson was a prominent scholar and administrator, no one knew whether he would make a successful governor. In order to campaign, he had to resign his position at Princeton. And what would happen if he lost the election? He would also have

Ellen Wilson photographed when her husband was the governor of New Jersey

Woodrow Wilson photographed around 1910

lost his job at the university. But Wilson was a quietly determined man. Losing was not part of his scheme.

On election day 1910, Wilson won by some 50,000 votes. As governor, he came to be respected. He was an honest man, and his earlier administrative duties at Princeton helped him understand how to run a state. He was a successful governor who brought about many lasting changes. So many people admired him that it seemed the next step would be for Wilson to run as the Democratic candidate in the 1912 presidential election.

Wilson Becomes President

The 1912 presidential election was a three-way race. Wilson was the Democratic candidate running against two former presidents. William Howard Taft was the Republican incumbent. Taft's predecessor, Theodore Roosevelt, ran on the Bull Moose party ticket. Although the split in the ticket helped Wilson to win, his victory was not overwhelming. He received only 42 percent of the popular vote, but his electoral college victory was a landslide.

Woodrow Wilson was inaugurated on March 4, 1913, as the 28th president of the United States. His wife and three daughters were by his side on inauguration day.

A president's inaugural address usually sets the tone of a new administration. Wilson called for reform in his first inaugural address, citing "inexcusable waste" in government and private life and criticizing those people who had used the government for "private and selfish purposes." He called for a return to the ideals of the founders of the nation. His program came to be known as the "New Freedom."

Almost as soon as he was inaugurated, Wilson held a scheduled news conference. It was the first time such an event had taken place. He felt that it was important for the press, as a group, to be given necessary information about the country's policies. The tradition has continued to the present day.

Although the amendment to the Constitution legalizing an income tax had been passed by Congress under Taft in 1909, it was not ratified by three-fourths of the states until February of 1913. In September of the same year Wilson was instrumental in getting a new tariff bill passed. Wilson was also responsible for legislation that helped to bring the chaotic banking system under control. Currency reform was established when a centralized system of regional federal banks was set up. These banks were coordinated and regulated by the federal government.

In 1914 the problem of enormous companies taking an unfair share of profits was corrected. In that year the Clayton Antitrust Act was signed. This law was designed to prevent abuses by companies that tried to monopolize business.

The Wilson White House

The Wilsons quickly renovated the White House living quarters. They were quite happy remaining upstairs in their new home. The Wilsons much preferred being together as a family to entertaining visiting dignitaries.

Seemingly a withdrawn man, Wilson was apparently relaxed and fun-loving with his family. But in public he gave the sense of being very shy, even aloof. In fact, he was a complex intellectual who did not let people get close to him easily. He also had a stubborn character and seemed unwilling or unable to compromise.

The family was a close one, and the three daughters all shared a good sense of humor. The Wilson daughters were in their 20s when the family moved into the White House. Stories are told of the daughters joining sightseeing tours of visitors to the White House. Frequently they would complain to the other people on the tour about how poorly President Wilson was running the country. Needless to say, the tourists didn't have a clue as to who was making these outrageous remarks!

Mrs. Wilson and her three daughters

Because she was a talented painter, Mrs. Wilson quickly found a room with a skylight in the White House attic. She converted this into a studio where she could pursue her painting.

Mrs. Wilson also beautified the White House grounds with rosebushes and trees as well as box hedges. Ellen Wilson planted the first White House rose garden in 1913.

Although Ellen Wilson enjoyed nothing as much as painting, she also made time for charities. As first lady, Mrs. Wilson shunned the rigors of social life—the teas and receptions—and concerned herself with human social issues.

Mrs. Wilson also set up a room in the White House where arts and crafts produced by women from the mountains of North Carolina and Tennessee could be displayed. Sales of these handcrafted products helped the women support their families.

Mrs. Wilson was instrumental in securing passage of a much-needed slum clearance act. She invited legislators to go with her on a tour of the urban slums around Washington, D.C. They witnessed the squalor in which large numbers of the poor were forced to live. Many Washington streets and alleys were cluttered with shacks, tents, and lean-tos where the poor lived without heat, water, or electricity.

During his White House years, Wilson enjoyed playing billiards. In fact, he enjoyed the game so much that Mrs. Wilson had a billiards room installed in the executive mansion. Eventually even the Wilson daughters came to like the game. Wilson also played golf, but not very well.

Two of the three Wilson daughters were married in the White House. In November 1913 Jessie was married to Francis (Frank) Sayre in the East Room. The wedding was considered one of the season's most glittering social events. But the bridegroom almost didn't make it to his own wedding. He had come directly from the Virginia shore and was not carrying an invitation to the wedding or any proof of his identity. Security was tight, and Sayre had a hard time convincing guards that he belonged *inside* the White House.

Eleanor (Nell) was married in the spring of 1914 to Wilson's secretary of the treasury, William G. McAdoo. But because of her mother's failing health, Nell's wedding in the Blue Room was a much smaller and quieter affair than her sister's had been.

Wilson was a devoted husband to his wife and father to his three daughters. But in August 1914 his beloved Ellen died. Almost a year earlier, Mrs. Wilson had fallen in the White House. She suffered from tuberculosis and Bright's disease, a deterioration of the kidneys. She rested and seemed to get better, but in fact her kidney disease was incurable. The Wilsons had shared nearly 30 years together, and Wilson was bereft by his wife's death.

Ellen Wilson was 54 when she died, having served as first lady for only one and a half of the eight years her husband was president. To date, no other first lady has died in the executive mansion.

Edith Bolling photographed when she was in boarding school

The Second Mrs. Wilson

Wilson was a lonely man after Ellen Wilson's death. Even his daughters could not console him. He read and played golf with friends, but did so with no joy.

Shortly after Ellen's death, however, Wilson met a Washington widow, Edith Bolling Galt, who relieved his loneliness. Mrs. Galt was a friend of Woodrow Wilson's cousin, Helen Bones. She and Wilson met by accident one day when Mrs. Galt accompanied Miss Bones to the White House for tea. Mrs. Galt was assured that Mr. Wilson was away, playing golf. By chance, of course, Wilson returned early to the White House. The couple met and were very taken with each other. It was the first time the president had smiled in months.

After a brief courtship, Wilson asked Mrs. Galt to marry him. For several months she turned him down. But in September she accepted his proposal. The couple was married in a quiet ceremony in December 1915. When they met, Mrs. Galt was 43 and Wilson was a youthful 58.

The second Mrs. Woodrow Wilson had been born Edith Bolling in Virginia in 1872. She came from a cultured family that had lost its money during the Civil War. Her father was a judge, and the girl was tutored at home by her paternal grandmother. At 15 she was able to attend public school, and at 16 she was sent to school in Richmond, Virginia.

A photograph of Woodrow Wilson and Edith Galt, taken just before their 1915 marriage

Edith Bolling moved to Washington, D.C., as a young woman, and in 1896 she married Norman Galt, a jeweler. In 1903 the couple had a son who died soon after his birth. In 1908 her happy marriage ended when her husband died.

Although Mrs. Galt had almost no business experience, she undertook to keep her husband's business going. Mrs. Galt took charge and kept the company successful until she sold the business for a handsome profit.

Mrs. Wilson was a large, outgoing woman with a take-charge attitude. Although she was childless, she showered those around her with a protective love that can best be described as maternal.

Christmas of 1915 was an especially happy time for Wilson. Wilson had been a widower for a little more than a year. Both he and Mrs. Galt wanted their marriage ceremony to be a private one. The wedding took place in Washington on December 18. The couple then took a train to Hot Springs, Virginia, and spent a brief honeymoon there. By January 3, 1916, the news from Europe—where war was raging—was not good. So the newlyweds rushed back to Washington.

Wilson's Second First Lady

Edith Wilson moved into the White House with her bedroom furniture and fittings, her beloved piano, her books, and her sewing machine. She quickly cleared away some of the first Mrs. Wilson's personal things. It was said that for exercise Edith rode a bicycle through the White House corridors.

When World War I started, the first lady led congressmen's wives in setting up sewing circles to make shirts and pajamas. The clothing was then distributed by the Red Cross to soldiers fighting in Europe.

During the war, many of the White House caretakers had gone to Europe to fight. Because help was scarce, Edith Wilson had a flock of sheep brought in to keep the grass trim

The newlyweds

on the White House lawns. As well, 90 pounds of fleece was auctioned off during Wilson's second term. Selling the fleece raised $100,000, which was donated to the Red Cross.

Although he was a staunch Christian, Wilson usually wanted to spend Christmas in nonreligious ways. He often played golf or even went to the theater. Edith Wilson insisted, however, that they go to church on Christmas. In 1917 the family went to the theater on Christmas Day. They then returned to the White House for a small dinner for 20.

At the start of his first term, Wilson had actually been able to go to Washington department stores and do his own Christmas shopping. But with World War I, security surrounding the president increased. He could no longer go about freely, and guards were stationed outside the White House. During the war the White House was virtually closed. Public dinners and receptions were canceled. For security reasons the doors were barred to the public from 1917 until 1921.

When the 1916 presidential election came around, most people felt that Wilson, having kept the country out of war, deserved to be reelected. And he was, but just barely. Both the popular vote and the electoral college vote over Republican Charles Evans Hughes were narrow. Edith Wilson helped her husband campaign during the 1916 election. Her role was an indication of what was to come.

Wilson was delighted that he could continue working. A great loner, he rarely consulted his cabinet members or set up meetings of advisers. At no point did his White House staff number more than 40. World War I was partly responsible for making the president remote from the people. But in many ways he created the sense of isolation at the White House himself.

Wilson was a perfectionist who wanted to do everything himself. He had difficulty delegating tasks to others. As a consequence, he often drove himself to the point of exhaustion.

Throughout the war Wilson maintained his grueling schedule of 18-hour workdays. He composed all his own speeches, correspondence, and memoranda. He usually drafted them in shorthand and then transcribed them himself on a typewriter.

In 1915 Wilson's first grandchild was born in the White House. And in the same year Wilson made the first transcontinental phone call from the Oval Office. Despite

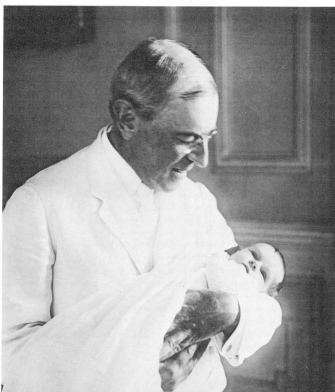

Wilson proudly displays his firstborn grand-daughter, Ellen Wilson McAdoo.

29

new inventions such as the telephone and the automobile, Wilson maintained old-fashioned values. For instance, Wilson disliked the telephone so much that he instructed the operators not to interrupt him with a call, no matter how urgent it was.

In January 1918, with war still raging, Wilson made a speech to the Senate asking for a proposed League of Nations. It was the beginning of what would come to be known as Wilson's Fourteen Points.

During most of Wilson's White House term, women were not allowed to vote. Those women who protested, and wanted the vote, were called suffragettes. Frequently they marched outside the White House demonstrating in order to make their wishes known.

Edith Wilson found the women's rights movement distasteful and the activists unfeminine. The only one of her husband's speeches that Edith did not enjoy was an address he gave at a meeting of suffragettes. Wilson did not believe in their cause either. But he was finally forced to recognize that times were changing. He recommended the 19th amendment to the Constitution. Proposed in 1919 and ratified in 1920, this amendment extended voting rights to women.

Wilson and other world leaders just before the Treaty of Versailles is signed

The President
Goes to Europe

World War I ended on November 11, 1918. The day was celebrated for many years as Armistice Day (it is now known as Veterans Day). More than 100,000 Americans had been killed, and some 200,000 were wounded.

Shortly after, on December 3, 1918, President and Mrs. Wilson boarded a train and left Washington. They traveled to New Jersey, where they climbed aboard the *George Washington*. Once a luxury liner, the great ship had been pressed into service as a troopship during the war. The Wilsons sailed on it to France. Woodrow Wilson was the first president to visit Europe while in office.

Wilson went to help negotiate the peace treaty that was to decide what would happen now that the war was over. He wanted to present his fourteen-point plan personally at the peace conference in Paris. Wilson believed strongly that war was evil, and his fourteenth point was intended to allow for an organization to prevent wars from ever happening again. He called this the League of Nations.

While in Europe Mrs. Wilson visited schools and hospitals. Women were not allowed to attend the peace meetings. But arrangements were made for Mrs. Wilson to remain hidden behind heavy red curtains in a small anteroom next to the meeting room. In this way she could hear what was going on and witness the signing of the peace treaty.

Except for one brief visit to Washington, Wilson was gone until July 1919. It was not until June 28 that Germany finally agreed to sign the treaty. In the stately Hall of Mirrors at the Palace of Versailles outside Paris, the treaty ending World War I was signed.

The Hall of Mirrors at Versailles

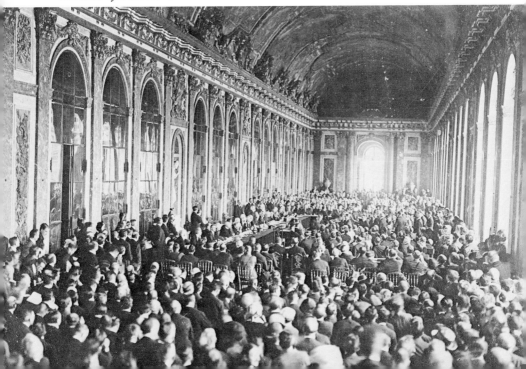

In 1919 Wilson spoke all over the country. Here he addresses a crowd in Baltimore.

Back from Europe

When Wilson came back to the United States, he found a country in unrest. There were food shortages and strikes. And American women, still unable to vote, were demanding the right to do so. Americans in general wanted nothing to do with Europe. No one really understood why more than 100,000 Americans had died fighting in countries far from home. Most Americans couldn't have cared less about the rest of the world.

The president had scored some points in Europe. A treaty ending the war had been signed. Even so, Wilson had been away a long time, and he was out of touch with the United States. And he was worn out. The months of negotiation had left him physically exhausted. A bout of influenza in 1918, followed by asthma attacks, produced insomnia that robbed him of strength. His doctors warned him that only complete rest would restore his health.

Wilson refused to obey his doctors' orders. He embarked on a speaking tour to convince Americans of the wisdom of the League of Nations. Wilson also knew he had to get a two-thirds majority vote in the Senate to approve the treaty's terms. And he felt the only way to get this support was to travel the country and press for world peace.

In his campaign to gain acceptance for the League of Nations, Wilson traveled 8,000 miles in 22 days, stopping in more than 40 cities. In most places he gave hour-long speeches, took part in parades, and attended political luncheons, dinners, and receptions. Mrs. Wilson was always at his side.

On September 25, 1919, an exhausted Wilson stumbled over words in a speech given in Pueblo, Colorado. The next morning, in Wichita, Kansas, he was unable to give another speech. His doctors ordered Wilson to return to Washington at once. There he suffered a stroke on October 2 from which he never fully recovered. The stroke paralyzed the left side of his body, which meant that he could barely move.

A White House without a President

The White House kept Wilson's illness a secret. For months the public was unaware of the seriousness of his disability. It was during this time that Mrs. Wilson took over many of the president's responsibilities. Some people whispered behind her back and called her "Mrs. President." Others referred to her as the "Iron Queen" and "America's First Woman President."

In December 1919 a crisis arose with Mexico. There seemed to be no alternative but to let Wilson's advisers meet with the president. They could see that he was obviously ill, but his mind was alert and he was familiar with the points of the issue. Although many people felt that Wilson should not remain in office, after that meeting no one questioned his ability.

Unquestionably Edith Wilson was her husband's most important adviser. After his stroke, she and the White House physician, Dr. Cary Grayson, protected the sick president. If the president was well enough, she consulted him on important issues. But much of the time he was too ill to be disturbed. Although many people feel that Mrs. Wilson ran the country, it is probably more accurate to say that no one ran it.

Even before Wilson's illness, Edith Wilson had a great deal of influence. During the war she was one of the people who knew many of the codes that were used to transmit secret messages to the powers in Europe.

Some thought that if Wilson were to resign, it would further injure his weak health. His doctors and his wife believed this strongly.

Seven months after his stroke, Wilson appeared at a cabinet meeting. He was greatly weakened and could walk only with difficulty.

Although by the spring of 1920 he still could not walk, Wilson seemed to be better. People thought he was getting stronger. It was another election year, and he wanted desperately to continue his peace work as president. But he was also realistic and knew that his chances for re-election were slim. In fact, the Democrats were trounced by Republican Warren G. Harding on election day. Ironically, Harding turned out to be a disaster. His presidential years were riddled with scandal.

Wilson's dream of American involvement in the League of Nations was also denied when the Senate blocked America's entrance. The treaty fell short by seven votes of the two-thirds majority needed for approval. A Republican majority blocked ratification of the treaty.

Despite his political setbacks at home, Wilson received a prestigious international honor. He was awarded the Nobel Peace Prize in December 1920. The award came to him largely through his efforts on behalf of the League of Nations.

An ailing man, Wilson was seldom seen by the public.

After the White House

In March 1921 the Wilsons left the White House. Before they departed, Edith Wilson turned over many of Ellen Wilson's most prized possessions to an auction house. These included Ellen's paintbrushes and her artist's pallette.

The Wilsons had decided to remain in Washington and moved to a specially equipped house. There was an elevator that Wilson could use to get around easily. Wealthy friends had made the purchase of the house possible.

Set in a part of Washington known as Embassy Row, the house, at 2340 S Street, was comfortable and elegant. Just five years old, it had all the latest conveniences, including a sun room overlooking the back garden. Servants' rooms and the kitchen were located in the basement.

Wilson's main intention in retirement was to write a book of memoirs. He wanted to share his years of public service. But Wilson also felt forgotten and ignored by the people he had served. Gradually his strength waned, and he never completed more than the dedication: to Edith Bolling Wilson.

In retirement, however, Wilson did bring out a book of essays on behalf of his favorite cause, the League of Nations. *The Road Away from Revolution* was published in 1923. It was one of many books that Wilson wrote in his lifetime. His writing had included several books on political science, a biography of George Washington, and a collection of literary essays. In 1902 he had published *A History of the American People*, a five-volume set.

Wilson's casket was carried to Washington's National Cathedral.

The couple led a quiet life in Washington. The former president never fully recovered from the effects of his stroke. On the morning of February 3, 1924, Wilson died. His wife and his daughter Margaret were at his side. Margaret Wilson was the only one of the daughters who never married. For a time she pursued a singing career. Then she worked in advertising and investments before turning to Indian mysticism.

An elaborate funeral ceremony was held at Washington's National Cathedral. In 1924 the cathedral was still not complete. Following the service, Wilson was buried in the church's basement. Wilson was the first president to be buried in Washington.

Edith Wilson survived her husband by almost 40 years. The S Street house remained her home. Not surprisingly, she worked on behalf of her husband's causes for many years. She continued to support the League of Nations, even though the United States never joined. Mrs. Wilson

Edith Wilson (seated) *remained a popular figure in Washington. She is pictured here with Bess Truman* (left) *and Eleanor Roosevelt* (right).

remained active and healthy until her death.

During World War II, Edith Wilson performed auxiliary functions such as sewing and knitting, just as she had during World War I. She remained a well-known figure in Washington and was often seen, particularly at important Democratic party functions.

In one of her last appearances, Edith Wilson rode in an open limousine at John F. Kennedy's inauguration in January 1961. She sat on the dais during Kennedy's swearing-in ceremony.

By the end of the year, though, at 88, Edith Wilson was gone. Her death occurred on December 28, 1961. It would have been Woodrow Wilson's 105th birthday.

Mrs. Wilson willed the S Street house as a gift to the nation through the National Trust. Wilson's bedroom has been left exactly as it was when he died.

The Wilson Legacy

Woodrow Wilson lived through one of the most eventful periods in U.S. history in a lifetime that began just before the Civil War. A Southerner, he experienced the rigors and humiliation of the Reconstruction period, as the states that lost the war were once again integrated into the Union.

And Wilson witnessed the western expansion that finally made the West and Southwest integral parts of the United States. Much of this growth was made possible by the country's rapid industrialization.

During Wilson's presidency an important domestic reform was a revision in the way senators are elected. The Constitution was amended so that senators are elected by the people. Before the ratification of the 17th Amendment in 1913, senators were chosen by state legislatures.

The early years of the 20th century and the emergence of the United States as a victor in World War I saw the rise of the United States as a world power. It was also the end of the great period of immigration that had brought an influx of Europeans to the United States in the late 19th and early 20th centuries.

Wilson was blessed in marrying two remarkable women. The two were very different. Both brought their talents and interests to the marriage, and both helped Wilson fulfill his destiny in many ways.

The first Mrs. Wilson was a gentle and scholarly wife and mother who served as a potent adviser and helped her husband reach his potential.

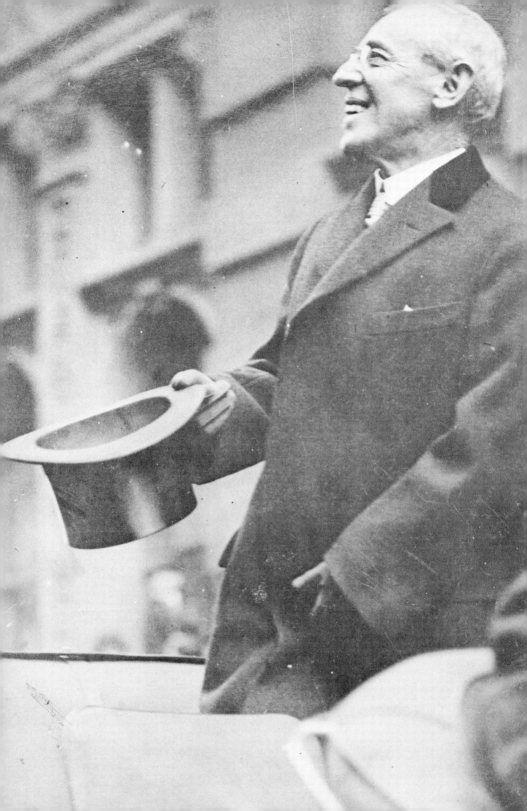

The second Mrs. Wilson was a strong maternal presence who comforted the grief-stricken widower reeling under the loss of his first wife. Edith Wilson guided her husband through nearly ten years that saw the strain of war, followed by the president's failing health and slackening powers. When the president was at his weakest, she virtually ran the country and piloted him through the completion of his second term.

Woodrow Wilson was a complex and many-sided man. He was one of the nation's visionaries. He recognized America's role as an international peacekeeper. Wilson was a man of peace, whose character had been forged by two great wars—the Civil War of his boyhood and World War I. He was also one of the great American presidents.

A quiet man, Wilson actually enjoyed public appearances.

For Further Reading

Anthony, Carl Sferrazza. *First Ladies: The Saga of the Presidents' Wives and Their Power, 1789-1961.* New York: William Morrow and Company, Inc., 1990.

Collins, David R. *Woodrow Wilson, 28th President of the United States.* Ada, Oklahoma: Garrett Educational Corporation, 1989.

Fisher, Leonard Everett. *The White House.* New York: Holiday House, 1989.

Friedel, Frank. *The Presidents of the United States of America.* Revised edition. Washington, D.C.: The White House Historical Association, 1989.

Giblin, James Cross. *Edith Wilson: The Woman Who Ran the United States.* New York: Viking, 1992.

Klapthor, Margaret Brown. *The First Ladies.* Revised edition. Washington, D.C.: The White House Historical Association, 1989.

Leazell, Perry. *Woodrow Wilson.* New York: Chelsea House, 1987.

Lindsay, Rae. *The Presidents' First Ladies.* New York: Franklin Watts, 1989.

The Living White House. Revised edition. Washington, D.C.: The White House Historical Association, 1987.

Osinski, Alice. *Woodrow Wilson.* Chicago: Childrens Press, 1989.

St. George, Judith. *The White House: Cornerstone of a Nation.* New York: G. P. Putnam's Sons, 1990.

Sandak, Cass R. *The White House.* New York: Franklin Watts, 1980.

Index